DC HEROES

BATMAN

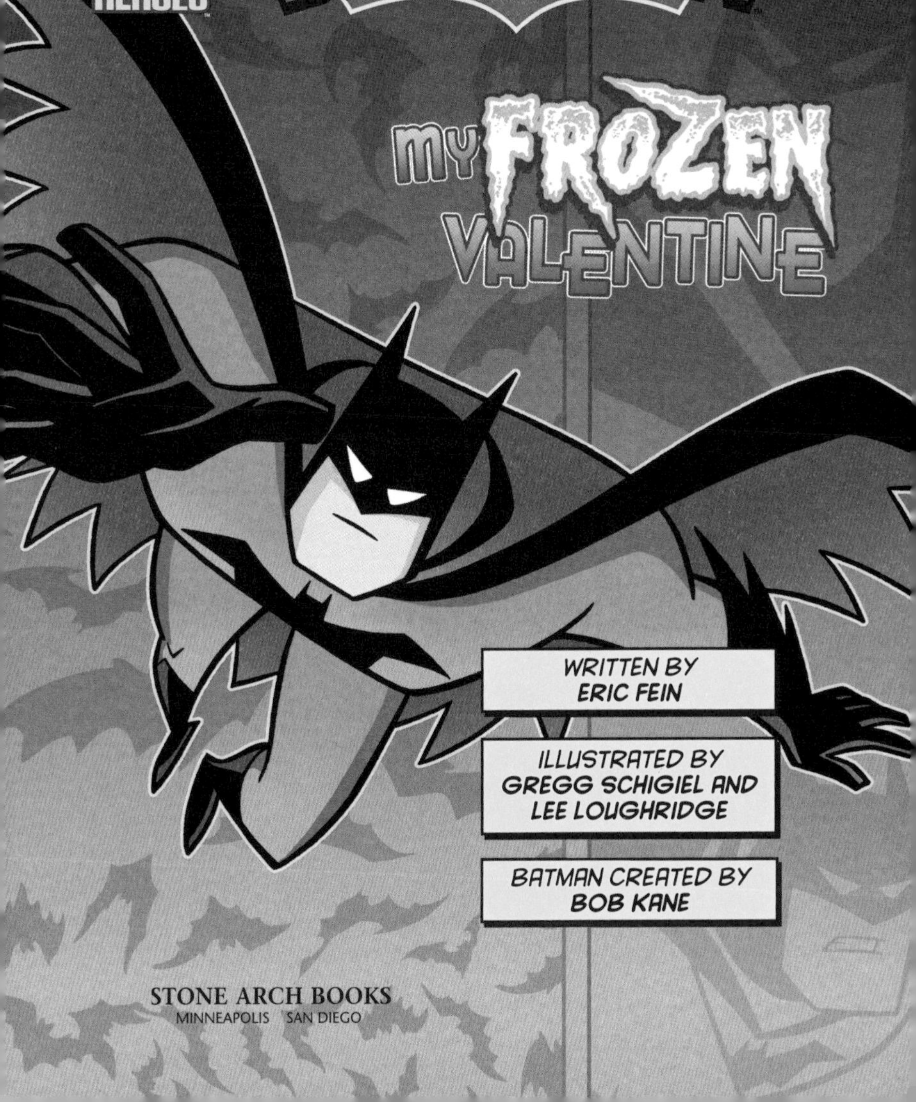

MY FROZEN VALENTINE

WRITTEN BY
ERIC FEIN

ILLUSTRATED BY
GREGG SCHIGIEL AND
LEE LOUGHRIDGE

BATMAN CREATED BY
BOB KANE

STONE ARCH BOOKS
MINNEAPOLIS   SAN DIEGO

Published by Stone Arch Books in 2010
1710 Roe Crest Drive
North Mankato, Minnesota 56003
www.capstonepub.com

Library of Congress Cataloging-in-Publication Data

Fein, Eric.
  My frozen valentine / by Eric Fein ; illustrated by Gregg Schigiel.
    p. cm. -- (DC super heroes. Batman)
  ISBN 978-1-4342-1564-2 (lib. bdg.) -- ISBN 978-1-4342-1731-8 (pbk.)
  [1. Superheroes--Fiction.] I. Schigiel, Gregg, ill. II. Title.
  PZ7.F3337Mv 2010
  [Fic]--dc22
                                        2009006302

Summary: It's Valentine's Day in Gotham, but not everyone is celebrating.
Victor Fries (aka Mr. Freeze) has never gotten over the death of his wife,
Nora, and he's not about to let anyone enjoy this painful holiday. Only
Batman can stop the cold-hearted criminal before Victor refrigerates the
entire city!

Art Director: Bob Lentz
Designer: Bob Lentz

Printed in the United States of America in Stevens Point, Wisconsin.
042013
007349R

TABLE OF CONTENTS

CHAPTER 1

AN ICY CITY

Batman stood on the roof of Gotham City's Police Headquarters. **FLAP!** His cape whipped about in the freezing wind as though it were alive.

"Gotham City is not an easy place to live," Batman said. "And in a winter this harsh, the citizens of Gotham have grown even more desperate."

Police Commissioner James Gordon stood next to him, shivering. Gordon was Batman's only friend on the Gotham police force.

As the two men looked down at the street below, people hurried to and from buildings. Some of them wore two winter jackets to fight off the cold.

"The weather services can't explain the sudden drop in temperature," Gordon said, stuffing his hands deeper into his pockets. "The weather forecasts called for temperatures in the mid-50s."

"Instead, the temperatures have dropped so low that it hurts to breathe," Batman added.

"It's not just the cold temperatures," Gordon said. "We've been getting reports of strange objects hovering over the city. They look like flying saucers with some kind of weapon attached. One police officer said it was a cannon that fired rays of ice."

"This can only be the work of Victor Fries," Batman said. His voice sounded like a growl in the icy breeze.

"Mr. Freeze?" Gordon asked.

"Yes," Batman said. "Only Mr. Freeze has the technology to do something like this. It definitely matches his style, too."

"You're right," Gordon said.

"When is the mayor going to issue a warning to the public?" Batman asked.

"He is unwilling to do that without proof that this is a criminal act," Gordon said. "Today is Valentine's Day. He won't give people bad news on a major shopping day. He says it's bad for business."

"So is a city filled with frozen people," Batman said. Before Gordon could respond, he noticed something in the sky.

"Look!" Gordon said. An ice saucer was speeding toward them. It looked like a flying, silver disc. Small ice cannons were mounted underneath. Suddenly, the weapon fired at Gordon. **ZZRRRRTT!**

Batman shoved Gordon out of harm's way. The ice rays barely missed him.

Batman got to his feet and threw two Batarangs at the ice cannons. **CLANK! CLANK!** They damaged the cannons so they couldn't fire.

Unable to attack, the saucer began to speed away. Batman removed his grapnel gun from his Utility Belt. He aimed it at the saucer's belly and fired. **CLINK** The hook latched onto the saucer's underside.

"What are you doing?" asked Gordon.

"Hitching a ride," Batman replied.

As Batman jumped off the building, his cape spread out like giant bat wings. The saucer pulled him over the Gotham streets and buildings.

He used his free hand to hit a button on his Utility Belt, activating the Batmobile. He had parked the vehicle in a dark alley near police headquarters. The sleek black car roared to life and followed Batman through a tracking chip in his Utility Belt.

Batman pulled himself up the line and climbed onto the saucer. As he bent down to examine the silver surface, a large panel began to slide open. Then a wide view screen popped up. A face appeared.

It was Mr. Freeze!

"Good evening, Batman," Mr. Freeze said. "I see you have come out to play."

CHAPTER 2

FROZEN VOWS

Batman scowled. "What's your game this time, Freeze?" he asked.

"It's Valentine's Day," said Freeze. "I intend to share what is left of my heart with Gotham City. The events that turned me into Mr. Freeze robbed me of my wife, Nora. Since I cannot be with her, why should the people of Gotham be with *their* loved ones? By the end of the night, Gotham will know my pain. They will be caught between a rock and a hard place. I will turn this city into a frozen wasteland."

"But now we must part," Freeze added. "We both have busy nights ahead of us."

Without warning, the saucer flipped upside down, sending Batman tumbling toward the icy streets below.

Batman only had a few seconds before he would hit the ground. He twisted around so that he was facing the street. Then he spread his arms and grasped the edges of his cape with his hands. He was no longer falling. Now, he was gliding above the streets of Gotham.

He spotted the Batmobile stopped at a red light. He pressed a button on his Utility Belt. **CLICK!** The car's roof slid open. Batman changed his position and dropped down into the car. **CLICK!** The roof slid back into place.

When the light turned green, Batman hit the gas. VROOOOOM! The Batmobile sped into the night.

As he drove, Batman activated the connection to the computer in the Batcave. "Computer on," he said.

"Activated," replied the computer's electronic voice.

Batman knew he had no time to lose. He thought of what Mr. Freeze had said about Valentine's Day.

"Search Gotham news media outlets," Batman said. "Search terms are 'Valentine's Day events.'"

"Searching," the computer said.

After a few moments, the computer replied, "Search complete. Found 1,246 results."

Batman wouldn't be able to investigate all of the entries. He needed to narrow the field. He thought again about what Mr. Freeze had said. What did he mean by "between a rock and a hard place?" The saying meant being stuck in a bad position. However, "rock" also had another meaning. *Diamonds!* Batman smiled.

"Computer," he said. "Screen results with the word 'diamonds.'"

"Gotham Diamond Exchange is hosting a Valentine's Day event," the computer said. "One hundred million dollars in diamonds will be on display in celebration of the Exchange's 50th anniversary. Fifty couples will be married, and each will receive a diamond ring as a wedding gift."

"Those people are in danger," Batman said. "I'd better get moving."

The Diamond Exchange was housed in an old building in downtown Gotham. A giant sign hung across its entrance. It read: "Welcome to the Valentine's Day Wedding Celebration!"

News reporters and photographers lined the street. They interviewed and photographed the lucky couples as they entered the building. Armed guards stood at the entrance. They prevented anyone from getting inside who did not have a ticket.

Inside the main showroom, the brides and grooms took their positions. The center of the room glowed from all of the diamonds, which were in a special glass display case. There were hundreds of them stacked in small piles. Many of the diamonds were as large as walnuts.

All of the brides and grooms faced a stage that had a microphone on a stand. The head of the Diamond Exchange, Reginald Granger, stepped up to it.

"Good evening, ladies and gentlemen," Granger said. "We are all gathered here tonight to observe a special moment in your lives, as well as our 50th anniversary. We at the Diamond Exchange want to make your wedding day very special in celebration of this event. Each bride will be given a special diamond ring from the Exchange as a wedding gift."

Granger continued, "Now, let me introduce you to Hamilton Hill, the mayor of Gotham City. He will lead the wedding service."

Everyone cheered. However, the cheering was soon cut short. KRASSSHHH!

The doors to the showroom were blown off their hinges! Mr. Freeze and his men walked through the archways. Snow and ice fell around them.

"Good evening," Mr. Freeze said. "Sorry to interrupt, but the plans have been changed. There will be no celebrations tonight for any of you."

Mr. Freeze raised his ice gun. People screamed and panicked. Some tried to run for cover, but there was nowhere to hide.

ZZZRRRRTT! Mr. Freeze pulled the trigger. The beam struck a groom, and he was instantly encased in solid ice. Each time Mr. Freeze pulled the trigger, another person was frozen.

A few moments later, all of the brides and grooms looked like ice statues.

"Lennie, George," Freeze said, "load our frozen friends into the truck."

"Yes, sir," Lennie said.

Next, Freeze turned to the display case. **BZZT!** Once again he fired his ice gun, covering the case with a thick layer of ice. Then he turned toward one of his men.

"Otto," Mr. Freeze said. "Collect the diamonds."

"My pleasure," Otto said. He grabbed a large hammer and swung it as hard as he could. **CRUNCH!** The frozen glass shattered into hundreds of tiny pieces.

Then Otto and Arnie grabbed up the diamonds and put them into their bags. As Mr. Freeze watched them work, an icy smile came to his lips.

CHAPTER 3

MR. FREEZE WINS

"We got twenty couples loaded into the truck, boss," George said. "It won't take us much longer to load the rest."

"Good," Freeze said.

Suddenly, a dark shadow fell over them. **CRASH!** They looked up to see the skylight shatter.

Batman emerged from the skylight with his cape spread wide. Two of Freeze's men began to pull out their weapons as the Dark Knight descended on them.

THUD! Batman landed on top of the thugs and knocked them down. As Batman landed, he rolled to the ground. Then he flipped to his feet and stood tall in front of Mr. Freeze.

"Very impressive," said Mr. Freeze. "But now it's my turn."

ZZRRRRTT! He raised his ice gun and fired. Batman dodged the blast and rolled behind a table. Freeze fired at the table and froze it into a block of ice.

From behind the table, Batman removed three pill-shaped objects from his Utility Belt. He threw them over the table. They landed hard against the floor and snapped open.

Thick, green smoke immediately poured out of the capsules and filled the room.

While Freeze's men panicked, Batman sprang into action. Blinded by the smoke, Otto fired his weapon recklessly. Like a ghost, Batman stepped out of the smoke and knocked Otto out. Batman picked up Otto's gun and effortlessly snapped it in half. **KRAK!**

Batman hated guns. As a child, he lost his parents to a criminal with a gun. He promised himself he would never use them.

Batman leaped over the frozen guests. This brought him next to the other two men. They were standing back-to-back with their guns raised. Even through the smoke, Batman could see the fear in their eyes.

"Can you see him?" George said.

"No," Arnie said. "Where is he?"

"Right here," Batman growled.

Arnie and George both turned and screamed like children. Their shouts were cut short when Batman bounced their heads together. **CRAAAAACK!** They fell to the floor in a heap.

The smoke was clearing. Batman could see the blue glow of Mr. Freeze's armor in front of him.

"A delightful display, Batman," Freeze said. "Sadly, it won't matter in the long run. By tomorrow, Gotham will be covered in ice. My ice saucers will see to that."

ZZRRRRTT! Freeze fired his ice gun at Batman. The Dark Knight flipped out of the line of fire. Then he dived to his right behind a table. The ice ray just missed him.

Batman grabbed a large coffeepot off the table and threw it at Mr. Freeze.

Mr. Freeze ducked out of the way. The pot exploded against the wall behind him. A splash of hot coffee hit Freeze on his back. His suit began to crackle from the mix of hot and cold.

Mr. Freeze blasted the giant crystal chandelier that hung from the ceiling of the showroom. **KRASSSHHH!** It fell on top of Batman before he could jump to safety. Meanwhile, George and Arnie got back to their feet.

"Hey, boss," George yelled. "I hear police sirens. We have to get out of here now!"

Mr. Freeze frowned. "Very well," he said.

Freeze and his men headed toward the entrance to the showroom.

"What about Otto?" Lennie said. "We can't just leave him behind."

"You are correct," Mr. Freeze said. "We can't have him telling Batman where to find us."

Mr. Freeze spotted Otto at the far end of the room. He was still unconscious. Mr. Freeze blasted him with his ice gun.

Otto was now trapped in a block of ice.

"That will keep him from talking," Mr. Freeze said.

•   •   •

It took Batman several minutes to free himself from the heavy chandelier. Then he contacted his butler, Alfred, at Wayne Manor with a special communications device inside his mask.

"Alfred," he said.

"Yes, Master Bruce?" Alfred responded. The butler knew Batman's true identity as the millionaire Bruce Wayne.

"Contact Lucius Fox at Wayne Enterprises," Batman said. "Tell him that Mr. Wayne wants him to send the contents of Room 7D to the Gotham Diamond Exchange."

"At once, sir," Alfred said. "Are you hurt, Master Bruce?"

"I'll live," Batman said. "Just tell Fox to hurry. There are a lot of innocent people here whose lives are depending on that chemical."

CHAPTER 4

INSIDE THE BATCAVE

"It's going to take most of the night," the doctor said, "but the people Mr. Freeze left behind should thaw out safely."

The doctor was standing outside the Gotham Diamond Exchange with Batman, Commissioner Gordon, and Lucius Fox.

"Wayne Enterprises is happy to help the citizens of Gotham," Fox said.

"We're lucky that your company was developing this cure," Gordon said.

"It wasn't by chance," Fox replied.

"After Mr. Freeze's first attack on Batman months ago, Mr. Wayne had us work on a cure," Fox said.

"Batman, you said Freeze promised to cover all of Gotham in ice," Gordon said. "Can he do it?"

"Yes," replied Batman. "So, the sooner we find him, the better the chance we'll have to stop him."

"What about the twenty brides and grooms he kidnapped?" Gordon asked.

"They should be safe for the time being," said Batman. "Freeze didn't seem to want to hurt them. He just wants everyone to be as unhappy as he is."

Two medics passed by carrying a thawed-out Otto on a stretcher.

"Excuse me," Batman said to the medics.

"I need a moment with your patient," Batman said. The medics set the stretcher down on the street and stepped away. Batman kneeled down next to Otto.

"We need to talk," Batman said.

"I got nothing to say," Otto said, turning his head away.

Batman frowned. He leaned closer and said, "Are you sure about that?"

Otto turned to face the Dark Knight. He swallowed hard as Batman glared at him.

Batman growled, "Where is Freeze's hideout? Tell me!"

"Don't let him hurt me!" Otto cried.

Batman sighed. He noticed Otto was wearing gray overalls. Batman pulled out a pair of scissors from his Utility Belt.

"What are you doing?" Otto asked.

"If you won't talk, then your clothes will," Batman said. He leaned forward and snipped a one-inch square of cloth from Otto's overalls. Then he placed the piece of cloth in his Utility Belt.

A short time later, Batman was in the Batcave, deep below Wayne Manor. Even with his mask off, Bruce Wayne's face lost none of its intensity.

Bruce sat at the workstation in front of his computer. He placed the cloth square under a scanner. Alfred stood next to him.

"Running a test, sir?" Alfred asked.

"Exactly," Batman said. "It will tell me what chemicals are in the fabric. That should help me narrow down the possible locations for Freeze's hideout."

The computer spoke, "Scan complete. High amounts of Freon detected."

An exact chemical breakdown of Freon was displayed on the computer's screen. Bruce leaned forward, deep in thought. He began to type. Next, the computer displayed a map of Gotham City. Three dots glowed on the map.

"What do those dots mean?" Alfred said.

"Freon is used by refrigerator factories," Batman said. "I searched Gotham for those types of businesses. Then I narrowed the search to factories that had closed. It gave me three results, which are seen on the map. One factory burned down last year. Another is near a busy park — Freeze wouldn't have a hideout there."

"And this third one?" Alfred asked.

"The third one," Batman said, "belongs to a company called Freeze Rite. It's in an isolated area overlooking Gotham Harbor."

"Sounds like the perfect place for a hideout," Alfred said.

"Agreed," Batman said. "Computer, upload the Freeze Rite blueprints to the computer in the Batboat."

"Upload complete," the computer said.

Batman hurried down a flight of stairs to an underground river. The Batboat was docked there.

"Don't wait up for me, Alfred," Bruce said. "It's going to be a long, cold night."

•   •   •

Mr. Freeze and his men were deep inside the Freeze Rite refrigerator factory.

George stared at the diamonds spread out on a workbench. He gathered a handful of the gems. "What a score!" he said.

George, Lennie, and Arnie couldn't stop playing with the glittering rocks.

"We're rich, boss!" Arnie said.

"I care nothing for wealth," said Mr. Freeze. "The diamonds are just icing on the cake. The real victory will be the destruction of Gotham City."

"Whatever you say, boss," George said.

Mr. Freeze walked into a nearby room that he called the ice garden.

The frozen brides and grooms stood on silver bases. They were spread out in rows. Each face was frozen in terror.

A smile crackled across Freeze's lips.

BEEP! BEEP! Suddenly, a red light blinked behind him. Freeze walked toward his icy computer.

Security cameras were connected to the computer. They monitored the area outside the factory. As one of the cameras zoomed in, the screen showed the Batboat speeding across Gotham Harbor toward the factory.

Mr. Freeze pushed a button on the control panel.

Deep within the factory, engines hummed to life. The computer screen flashed. In an electronic voice, it said, "Ice saucers activated."

Mr. Freeze smiled. Batman was going to get an icy welcome.

CHAPTER 5

THE BAT ATTACKS

The Batboat sliced through the waves in Gotham Harbor toward the factory up ahead. Suddenly, the computer said, "Warning! Unknown objects approaching!"

Batman looked up to see two ice saucers flying right at him. **ZZRRRRTT!** They opened fire. The river began to fill with large chunks of ice. Batman expertly steered around the dangerous ice blocks.

Suddenly, an ice saucer flew so low that it almost hit the Batboat. Batman fired his grapnel gun at it. **CHING!**

The hook hit the ice saucer on its edge, sending it spinning out of control. It crashed into the other saucer.

There was a flash of light. The first saucer fell into the river. The other fell on the Batboat, pushing it underwater.

The water was freezing, but that was the least of Batman's worries. The Batboat was sinking! Batman pressed a button on the boat's computer. Metal plates began clicking into place. The Batboat was changing into a submarine. Batman aimed the vehicle toward the shore.

• • •

Inside the factory, Arnie, Lennie, and George were eating sandwiches and watching a hockey game on television. Suddenly, they heard the saucers crash.

"What's going on out there?" Arnie asked. "Was that an explosion?"

"Lets get out of here!" George said. "Freeze can take care of himself."

"Good idea," Lennie said.

They ran out of the room and down the hall. As they neared the factory's rear door, a Batarang flew in front of them.

CRUNCH! It shattered the only lightbulb in the hall. Now they were surrounded by darkness.

"It's Batman!" George yelled.

George pulled out a small flashlight and spun around in a circle. Arnie and Lennie had disappeared. Instead, the beam from his light fell on Batman.

"Boo," Batman whispered.

George stumbled backward in surprise. He fell to the floor. Before he could get up, Batman slapped a pair of handcuffs on him. **CLICK!**

"What did you do with Arnie and Lennie?" George asked.

Batman pointed his own flashlight to the other side of the hall. Arnie and Lennie were both tied up. They were dangling by their jackets from a couple of hooks in the concrete wall.

"They're just hanging around," Batman said. "Now behave while I go take care of your boss."

The Dark Knight moved down the hall like a living shadow. Soon, Batman reached the ice garden. Mr. Freeze was waiting for him.

"You have more lives than a cat," Freeze said. He stood atop a large ice saucer.

"It's time to give up, Mr. Freeze," Batman said.

"What! Before I turn Gotham into my own ice kingdom?" Freeze said.

"Over my dead body!" Batman said.

"If you insist," said Freeze.

Batman leaped onto the silver saucer. It tilted from side to side as it rose toward a floor-to-ceiling window. Batman lunged at Freeze and grabbed the barrel of his ice gun just as Freeze pulled the trigger. The blast struck the window, turning it into a sheet of solid ice.

CRASH! The saucer smashed through the frozen window and soared into the night sky.

The saucer flew above Gotham's industrial area. Tall smokestacks rose up from the factories built around the harbor.

WHAM! Freeze elbowed Batman in the stomach. The blow knocked the Dark Knight backward, but he was able to grab onto the edge of the saucer.

"Fight all you want, Batman," Freeze said, standing over him. "It will make no difference. You will end up frozen just like the others."

As Freeze lifted his foot to strike, Batman swung his legs and flipped back onto the saucer. Swiftly, Batman did a sweep kick, knocking Freeze onto his back.

Anger boiled within the icy villain. He lunged at Batman. **SLAM!** Batman was knocked onto his back.

It was a reckless move. The saucer was now high above the smokestacks, and a fall would probably be deadly. But Freeze didn't seem to care. All he wanted to do was destroy Batman.

ZZRRRRTT! Freeze opened fire again, but Batman rolled to avoid the blast. The beam hit the computer that controlled the saucer. The silver disk began to shake wildly.

BOOM! Smoke and flames burst out of the saucer, causing Freeze to stumble. He lost his footing and fell off of the saucer. He plummeted into a smokestack and disappeared without a sound.

Batman felt his feet slip. He grabbed his grapnel gun and aimed it at a nearby building. The hook latched onto the building, and Batman swung to safety.

Seconds later, the flaming saucer crashed into the harbor.

• • •

Back at the factory, Batman stood next to Commissioner Gordon. Mr. Freeze had been rescued. He was on his way back to his refrigerated cell in Arkham Asylum. The police had his henchmen in handcuffs.

Batman and Gordon smiled as the frozen brides and grooms were thawed out.

"Lucius Fox says they will be just fine," Gordon said. "And the Diamond Exchange rescheduled the wedding party. Once the couples have recovered, they will get to have their dream weddings after all."

"That's good news," Batman said. "It's enough to warm a cold heart on a winter's day."

Mr. Freeze

REAL NAME: Dr. Victor Fries

OCCUPATION: Professional Criminal, Scientist

BASE: Gotham City

HEIGHT:
6 feet

WEIGHT:
190 pounds

EYES:
Icy blue

HAIR:
None

Victor Fries felt lonely throughout his schooling. He was teased constantly by classmates and was sure he'd never have a friend. Then he met Nora, and everything changed. They fell in love. But when Nora became ill with an incurable disease, Victor lost hope. To say Mr. Freeze's heart went cold would be an understatement. His indifference toward human life is now so severe that he spreads suffering to anyone within his icy grasp. That way, other people will feel his pain.

G.C.P.D. GOTHAM CITY POLICE DEPARTMENT

- When Freeze's wife, Nora, became deathly ill, he froze her in a cryogenic chamber to preserve her. He had hoped to one day find a cure for her illness. However, in a struggle with Batman, he accidentally shattered her chamber, killing her. Mr. Freeze blames Batman for the tragic event, and seeks revenge against him.

- After being exposed to various chemicals, Mr. Freeze's body composition was forever changed. He requires constant refrigeration, or his lungs will melt and his blood will boil.

- The ice-based technology that Mr. Freeze uses requires the most perfect diamonds for fuel. Thus, many of his crimes involve the robbery of expensive diamond exhibits or jewelry stores.

- Mr. Freeze has the tools to match his icy schemes. He uses a freeze weapon that turns his enemies into blocks of ice. He also wears a cryogenic suit that chills him to the sub-zero temperature his body needs to survive. His suit also grants him strength and durability.

CONFIDENTIAL

BIOGRAPHIES

Eric Fein is a freelance writer and editor. He has edited books for Marvel and DC Comics, which included well-known characters such as Batman, Superman, Wonder Woman, and Spider-Man. Eric has also written dozens of graphic novels and educational children's books. He currently lives in New Jersey.

Gregg Schigiel is originally from South Florida. He knew he wanted to be a cartoonist when he was 11 years old. He has worked on projects featuring the characters Batman, Spider-Man, SpongeBob SquarePants, and just about everything in between. Gregg currently lives and works in New York City.

Lee Loughridge has been working in comics for more than 14 years. He currently lives in sunny California in a tent on the beach.

GLOSSARY

activated (AK-tuh-vate-id)—turned something on

chandelier (shan-duh-LEER)—a fancy light fixture that hangs from a ceiling

descended (di-SEND-id)—lowered or climbed down

examine (eg-ZAM-uhn)—look carefully at something

industrial (in-DUHSS-tree-uhl)—an industrial area has lots of businesses and factories

investigate (in-VESS-tuh-gate)—to find out as much as possible about something

recklessly (REK-liss-lee)—carelessly and without considering the safety of others

shattered (SHAT-urd)—broke into tiny pieces

Utility Belt (yoo-TIL-uh-tee BELT)—Batman's belt, which holds all of his weaponry and gadgets

wasteland (WAYST-land)—a barren or empty area

DISCUSSION QUESTIONS

1. If you could have any of Batman's tools or inventions, which would you choose? His grapnel gun? His Utility Belt? The Batmobile? Why?

2. Batman uses his computer to research possible locations for Freeze's hideout. Discuss ways that you use computers at school and at home.

3. Mr. Freeze is angry and sad that he lost his wife, Nora. Does this make his behavior okay?

WRITING PROMPTS

1. Mr. Freeze was bullied a lot when he was younger. Have you ever been picked on? How did it make you feel? What did you do about it?

2. Imagine that a heat wave strikes Gotham City, and a super-villain is causing it. What is this villain's name? What abilities does he have? How will Batman fight him? You decide.

3. Batman drives his Batmobile, and Mr. Freeze pilots a silver saucer. Imagine you have your own super-vehicle. What does it look like? Write about it. Then, draw a picture of your vehicle.

MORE NEW BATMAN ADVENTURES!

ARCTIC ATTACK

CATWOMAN'S CLASSROOM OF CLAWS

HARLEY QUINN'S SHOCKING SURPRISE

THE MAN BEHIND THE MASK

THE PUPPET MASTER'S REVENGE

santa clara
county
library district

Renewals: (800) 471-0991

www.sccl.org

FROM THE PAGES
OF DC COMICS COMES...

SUPER DC HEROES

ORIGINAL, FULL-COLOR CHAPTER BOOKS!

IN THIS BOOK:

It's Valentine's Day in Gotham,
but not everyone is celebrating.
Victor Fries (aka Mr. Freeze)
has never gotten over the death
of his wife, Nora, and he's not
about to let anyone enjoy this
painful holiday.

Only Batman can stop the
cold-hearted criminal, before
Victor refrigerates the city!

$4.95 US $5.95

STONE ARCH BOOKS
Capstone Publishers • www.stonearchbooks.c
008-012 RL: 3.9 Guided Reading Level: M

BATMAN

DC
COMICS™
SUPER
HEROES

MANNING
DOESCHER
DeCARLO
LOUGHRIDGE

SCARECROW:
DOCTOR
OF FEAR